Chronicles of the Silent Hour

Oscar Wayne

Published by Oscar Wayne, 2024.

CHRONICLES OF THE SILENT HOUR

First edition. August 15, 2024.

ISBN: 979-8227050847

Written by Oscar Wayne.

Table of Contents

Chronicles of the Silent Hour

Chapter 1: *The Disappearance*

The small town of Whispers Creek was a place where the past seemed to linger in every shadow. Nestled in a secluded valley and surrounded by thick forests and rolling hills, the town had an eerie charm that both captivated and unsettled those who lived there. Cobblestone streets wound through rows of Victorian-era houses, and the old-fashioned town square had remained largely unchanged for over a century. The town's namesake, a narrow creek, whispered softly as it wound through the center, its waters flowing past moss-covered stones.

Seventeen-year-old Ivy Whitlock had called Whispers Creek home for her entire life, but the town had always held a certain mystery that intrigued her. With wavy, chestnut-brown hair that fell just past her shoulders and hazel eyes that were always searching for answers, Ivy was known for her inquisitive nature. Her slender frame and practical wardrobe—usually jeans, boots, and flannel shirts—belied the inner strength and determination that had grown within her over the years.

Despite the town's haunting beauty, Whispers Creek was a place tinged with sadness. The community had dwindled over the years, leaving behind an air of decay and abandonment. Many of the once-vibrant buildings were now boarded up or falling into disrepair, their windows shattered and walls covered in ivy. The few remaining residents were a tight-knit, secretive group, wary of outsiders and suspicious of anything that might disturb the fragile peace that had settled over the town.

At the heart of Whispers Creek stood the clock tower, an imposing structure that had long been a symbol of the town's history and its connection to time itself. The clock tower's rusted gears and cracked face were a haunting reminder of the town's past sins and the dark legacy that lingered within its borders.

Ivy had always been drawn to the mysteries of Whispers Creek. Her love for books and puzzles had fueled her passion for unraveling secrets, and the town's eerie atmosphere only deepened her curiosity

But when the disappearance of Lily Marks happened, Ivy's best friend since childhood. the mysteries of Whispers Creek took on a new, urgent meaning. Lily's absence left a void in Ivy's life, one that drove her to search for answers, no matter the cost. Lily was also seventeen, just a few months younger than Ivy, with her eighteenth birthday only weeks away. She had been full of plans for the future, talking excitedly about starting college in the fall and leaving Whispers Creek behind.

Lily had vanished without a trace, leaving behind only her backpack, carelessly abandoned on the edge of the woods. The town buzzed with rumors, and the once tranquil streets now hummed with fear. For Ivy, it was as if the very fabric of her life had been torn apart. Lily had been like a sister to her—they had shared everything, from secrets whispered late at night to dreams of escaping their small town.

The day Lily disappeared had been like any other. The two of them had spent the afternoon at their favorite spot by the river, talking about their future. Lily had seemed happy, more excited than ever about leaving for college. But when she didn't show up for dinner that night, Ivy knew something was wrong.

The next morning, Lily's parents had called the sheriff's office, frantic with worry. A search party combed the woods, but all they found was her backpack. No footprints, no signs of a struggle—just the bag, sitting eerily on the ground as if Lily had simply vanished into thin air.

As Ivy walked through the town's narrow streets that morning, she couldn't shake the feeling that something sinister was at play. She knew Lily better than anyone, and Lily would never have run away. Determined to find her friend, Ivy started her own investigation, Ivy found herself in the old town library, a place she had always considered a refuge. The library was a grand, dusty building with high, arched windows that let in beams of light, illuminating the countless rows of books that lined the shelves. But it wasn't the fiction or history sections that Ivy was interested in this time—it was the archives.

The archives were located in the basement of the library, a place where few ventured. The air was thick with the scent of aging paper and mildew, and the shelves were filled with old town records, newspapers, and files dating back over a century. Ivy spent hours digging through these records, her fingers stained with dust as she pored over every document that might offer a clue.

Among the old records, Ivy found missing persons reports that dated back decades, cases that had never been solved and were now long forgotten. She uncovered newspaper clippings about strange occurrences in Whispers Creek—stories of sudden disappearances, unexplained phenomena, and tragic accidents that seemed to defy logic. One report, from nearly a hundred years ago, detailed the mysterious vanishing of a young girl who had been last seen near the clock tower, her fate never discovered. The similarities to Lily's disappearance sent a chill down Ivy's spine.

But it wasn't just the old records that held clues—there were also things the police had overlooked. In their search for Lily, the local authorities had been thorough, but Ivy knew that they were also constrained by the limits of conventional investigation. They had focused on the obvious—questioning neighbors and searching the nearby woods. But they hadn't considered the deeper, more mysterious elements that Ivy believed were at play.

One night, Ivy reached the sheriff's station, her heart pounding with a mixture of apprehension and determination. She paused at the entrance, taking a deep breath before pushing the heavy door open. The smell of coffee and old wood greeted her as she stepped inside, the familiar sights and sounds of her father's domain grounding her in the moment. While sifting through dusty files in her father's office, Ivy found something strange—a diary, dated 1895, yet written in handwriting eerily similar to her own. The last entry was chilling:

"The Silent Hour is upon us. I must return before it finds me."

Beneath it was a sketch of a pocket watch, with the hands set to exactly 3:33 a.m.

Chapter 2: *The Clock Strikes 3:33*

Ivy's heart pounded as she stared at the diary. How could something over a century old bear her handwriting? And what did "The Silent Hour" mean?

Unable to sleep, Ivy sneaked out of her house at 3:00 a.m., driven by a gut feeling. She followed the path through the woods to where Lily's backpack had been found. The moon cast long shadows, and the trees whispered secrets in the wind.

At exactly 3:33 a.m., Ivy heard a faint ticking sound. She followed it, and there, nestled between the roots of an ancient oak, was an old pocket watch—just like the one in the diary. The hands were frozen at 3:33. As she touched the watch, the world around her began to spin, the trees and stars blurring into a whirlpool of color.

When the spinning stopped, Ivy found herself standing in the same woods, but something was different. The air was colder, and the trees seemed younger, their branches more gnarled and twisted. The familiar hum of distant traffic and the glow of streetlights were gone, replaced by an eerie silence and a thick fog that clung to the ground like a ghostly blanket.

She stepped out of the woods and gasped. Whispers Creek was gone, replaced by a town she barely recognized.

The quaint, modern houses with their manicured lawns and neat picket fences were nowhere to be seen. Instead, the streets were lined with Victorian-style homes, their facades dark and looming under the dim light of gas lamps that flickered in the mist. The cobblestone streets, slick with moisture, gleamed faintly in the moonlight, and the air smelled of coal smoke and damp earth.

Horse-drawn carriages clattered down the narrow roads, their wheels echoing ominously against the stone buildings. The townsfolk, dressed in heavy woolen coats, long skirts, and high-collared blouses, hurried past her with wary glances, their faces pale and drawn. Ivy noticed that many of the women wore bonnets, and the men sported top hats or bowler hats, their attire a stark contrast to the casual clothes she was used to seeing in Whispers Creek.

As she walked further into town, Ivy's heart raced with a mixture of fear and awe. The town square, which she had known all her life, was transformed. The fountain, usually surrounded by benches and colorful flower beds, was now a simple stone structure, its water frozen in the chilly night air. A solitary figure stood by the fountain, reading a newspaper by the light of a nearby lantern. The headline on the front page sent chills down her spine: *"Brutal Murder Rocks Whispers Creek: Young Girl Found Dead at 3:33 a.m."*

The article described a series of murders that had plagued the town in the summer of 1895, the very year Ivy had traveled to. Each victim was found at exactly 3:33 a.m., with no sign of struggle and no apparent cause of death. The locals whispered about a curse, a phantom killer who struck during "The Silent Hour."

As Ivy wandered through the town, she noticed other details that unnerved her. The familiar general store was now a small apothecary, its window display filled with glass jars containing strange herbs and powders. The bakery where her mother worked was instead a dusty library, its shelves lined with thick, leather-bound volumes. Even the air felt different—heavier, as if the town itself carried the weight of a dark secret.

Chapter 3: *The Murderer's Mark*

Ivy wandered the streets in a daze, trying to understand what had happened. The town was familiar yet foreign, every corner a distorted reflection of the place she had always known. But there was no time to dwell on the disorienting changes—she had to find out what was happening and, more importantly, how to get back to her own time.

The newspaper Ivy had seen detailed a horrifying murder, the latest in a string of killings that had plagued Whispers Creek in the summer of 1895. Each victim was found at exactly 3:33 a.m., their faces frozen in terror. The locals whispered about a curse, believing the killer was a malevolent spirit, striking without mercy.

Ivy had spent days combing through the old records in the library, piecing together fragments of history and rumors about the town's dark past. Desperate for answers, Yet, despite all the time she had spent digging through musty files and fading photographs, there were still too many gaps—too many unanswered questions. And those gaps led her to the one person in Whispers Creek who might hold the answers: Mrs. Beatrice Thatcher. Mrs. Thatcher was one of the town's oldest residents, a woman whose life spanned nearly a century. She was known among the townsfolk as a living repository of Whispers Creek's history—a keeper of stories and secrets long forgotten by others. For decades, Mrs. Thatcher had watched the town evolve, seen families come and go, and witnessed events that no one else could remember. Ivy had often heard her father speak of Mrs. Thatcher, describing her as a recluse who rarely left her old, creaky Victorian house at the edge of town. Some whispered that she was a witch, or that she knew things about the town that no one else should know.

On a dreary afternoon, Ivy gathered her courage and made her way to Mrs. Thatcher's home. The house was a grand but dilapidated structure, its once-ornate facade now weathered and overgrown with ivy. The garden was a tangled mess of wildflowers and weeds, and the iron gate creaked ominously as Ivy pushed it open. She walked up the stone path, her heart pounding in her chest as she approached the front door.

When she knocked, the sound echoed hollowly inside the house. A few moments later, the door creaked open, revealing Mrs. Thatcher standing in the dim hallway.

Mrs. Beatrice Thatcher was an imposing figure despite her age. She stood tall and straight; her thin frame draped in a long, dark dress that seemed to belong to another era. Her silver hair was pulled back into a tight bun, accentuating the sharp lines of her face. Deep wrinkles carved into her skin told the story of her many years, and her piercing blue eyes held a look of wisdom—and perhaps a touch of something else, something almost otherworldly.

"Miss Whitlock," Mrs. Thatcher greeted Ivy in a voice that was surprisingly strong for someone her age. It was clear from her tone that she had been expecting Ivy. "I wondered when you might come."

Ivy was taken aback. She hadn't anticipated that Mrs. Thatcher would know who she was or why she had come, but then again, Mrs. Thatcher was known for knowing things that others didn't.

"Yes, ma'am," Ivy replied, trying to steady her voice. "I... I need your help. My friend, Lily—she's gone missing, and I think you might know something about it. Something that the police don't."

Mrs. Thatcher's eyes softened ever so slightly, but there was a gravity in her expression that made Ivy's heart sink. The old woman stepped aside, motioning for Ivy to enter.

The inside of the house was dimly lit, with heavy curtains drawn across the windows. The air was thick with the scent of old wood and lavender, and the walls were lined with dusty bookshelves filled with ancient tomes and faded photographs. It was as if time had stood still within these walls, preserving the memories of a bygone era.

Mrs. Thatcher led Ivy to a small sitting room at the back of the house. The room was cluttered with antiques—ornate lamps, a porcelain clock, and a collection of strange trinkets that Ivy couldn't quite identify. They sat in silence for a moment, the weight of Ivy's request hanging in the air.

Mrs. Thatcher seemed to recognize the pocket watch immediately. Her eyes widened with fear as Ivy handed her the diary and the watch, both relics from another time.

"This diary belonged to my grandmother," Mrs. Thatcher whispered, her hands trembling as she traced the familiar lines of the handwriting. *"She was obsessed with finding the truth about The Silent Hour. But she disappeared before she could solve the mystery. The last time anyone saw her, she was holding a pocket watch just like this one."*

Mrs. Thatcher then told Ivy about a mysterious symbol known as the *Murderer's Mark*—a sinister sign that appeared near each crime scene, often overlooked by the untrained eye. The mark was a small, intricate engraving of a clock face with no hands, set into stone, wood, or even etched into glass. It was said to be the calling card of the killer, left behind as a taunt to those who dared to investigate the murders. The Mark was a warning, a sign that the killer had struck and would strike again.

Mrs. Thatcher led Ivy to her grandmother's old study, a room filled with yellowing papers, dusty books, and cryptic notes scrawled across the walls. In the center of the room was a large map of Whispers Creek, dotted with pins marking the locations of the murders. Each pin was accompanied by a rough sketch of the Murderer's Mark, drawn by Mrs. Thatcher's grandmother during her own investigation.

The Mark was always placed in hidden, obscure spots—underneath a window sill, carved into the base of a tree, or even embedded in the stonework of an old church. It was almost as if the killer wanted to make sure that only the most observant, the most desperate to find the truth, would ever see it.

Ivy's heart pounded as she realized she had seen something similar in her own time, near where Lily had disappeared. There had been a strange marking on the old oak tree, just a few feet from where Lily's backpack had been found. At the time, Ivy had dismissed it as an old carving, worn by the elements. But now, with Mrs. Thatcher's words echoing in her mind, she knew it had been the Murderer's Mark.

Determined to learn more, Ivy pored over the notes in the study, searching for a pattern, a clue that would help her understand how the killer operated. The notes described the Mark as a doorway—a symbol that allowed the killer to slip through time, leaving death and destruction in his wake. But the true nature of the Mark remained elusive, shrouded in mystery and fear.

As Ivy continued to search, she found an old, faded photograph tucked inside one of the books. The photograph showed a group of men standing in front of the town's clock tower, which looked much newer in the picture. One of the men, a tall figure with piercing eyes, stood apart from the others, his expression cold and distant. Ivy's breath caught in her throat as she noticed something in his hand—a pocket watch, identical to the one she had found in the woods.

The man's name was written on the back of the photograph: *Nathaniel Grayson*. According to Mrs. Thatcher's notes, Nathaniel had been a brilliant scientist in the late 1800s, obsessed with time and the mysteries of the universe. He had vanished under mysterious circumstances shortly before the murders began, and many believed he had died. But Ivy knew better now.

Nathaniel Grayson wasn't dead. He had unlocked the secret of time travel, and he was using it to exact a terrible revenge on the town that had wronged him.

As the pieces of the puzzle began to fall into place, Ivy realized with growing horror that the killer wasn't just someone from the past—it was someone who could travel through time, striking in different eras but always at 3:33 a.m. And now, that same killer was after her.

As Ivy rose to leave, Mrs. Thatcher placed a frail hand on her arm. "One more thing, Miss Morgan," she said softly. "Beware the Grayson mansion holds dark secrets."

But Ivy was determined to stop him. Armed with the pocket watch and the knowledge she had gained from Mrs. Thatcher; she knew she had to uncover the secrets of the Murderer's Mark and find a way to end Nathaniel's reign of terror before it was too late.

Chapter 4: *The Origins of Hatred*

Nathaniel Grayson was born in 1865, the only son of a wealthy family in Whispers Creek. His father, Edward Grayson, was a respected doctor, known for his pioneering medical practices. His mother, Eleanor, was a talented artist whose paintings hung in the grandest homes in the region. From a young age, Nathaniel was expected to follow in his father's footsteps, destined for greatness in the field of medicine.

But Nathaniel had other interests. His mind was drawn not to the human body, but to the mysteries of the universe. He was fascinated by the concept of time—how it flowed, how it could be measured, and whether it could be controlled. He devoured books on physics, astronomy, and philosophy, losing himself in theories of time travel and alternate dimensions. His obsession worried his parents, who hoped he would abandon his strange interests and focus on a more practical career.

Nathaniel was a prodigy. By the age of twenty, he had already published several papers on the nature of time, earning him a reputation as a brilliant but eccentric scholar. However, his theories were often dismissed by the scientific community, which viewed his ideas as outlandish and impossible. He was ridiculed by his peers and ostracized by the academic elite. This rejection only fueled his determination to prove them wrong.

In 1887, tragedy struck the Grayson family. Nathaniel's father contracted a mysterious illness that left him bedridden, unable to work or care for his family. Nathaniel, desperate to save his father, began experimenting with unorthodox methods, using his knowledge of time and physics to develop a machine he believed could manipulate time itself. He hoped to reverse the flow of time in his father's body, undoing the damage caused by the disease.

The town of Whispers Creek, already suspicious of Nathaniel's strange behavior, turned against him. Rumors spread that he was conducting dark experiments, meddling with forces beyond human comprehension. The townspeople, driven by fear and superstition, began to shun the Grayson family, refusing to seek Edward's medical services and boycotting Eleanor's artwork. The once-respected family became pariahs.

Nathaniel's experiments grew more desperate as his father's condition worsened. Late at night, strange lights and sounds emanated from the Grayson mansion, fueling the townspeople's fear. Some claimed to have seen Nathaniel in the cemetery, speaking to the dead, while others whispered that he had made a pact with dark forces in exchange for knowledge.

The breaking point came when Edward Grayson died in the spring of 1888. Nathaniel, consumed by grief and guilt, locked himself in his laboratory for days. When he finally emerged, he was a changed man. His obsession with time had taken a darker turn, and he was determined to make Whispers Creek pay for the suffering they had caused his family.

Nathaniel's hatred for the town grew as he uncovered more of its dark secrets. He discovered that his father's illness had been caused by contaminated water from a nearby river—polluted by a factory owned by the town's most powerful family, the Marstons. Edward Grayson had known about the contamination but had been threatened into silence by the Marstons, who feared the financial ruin that would follow if the truth came out. Nathaniel realized that the town had conspired to protect the Marstons at the expense of his father's life.

Betrayed by the town he had once called home, Nathaniel decided to use his knowledge of time to exact revenge. He perfected his time-travel device, a small, intricate machine that looked like an ordinary pocket watch but was capable of opening doorways in time. He would use it to travel to different eras, targeting the descendants of those who had wronged his family. Each time, he would leave behind the Murderer's Mark—a clock face with no hands, symbolizing the timelessness of his vengeance.

Nathaniel's first victim was a young woman named Amelia Marston; the daughter of the factory owner responsible for the pollution. On the night of her murder, the clock struck 3:33 a.m., and the town awoke to find her lifeless body in the town square. Her face was frozen in terror, with no sign of injury or struggle. The townspeople were horrified, and rumors of a curse began to spread.

But for Nathaniel, this was only the beginning. He traveled through time, striking at different points in Whispers Creek's history, always at 3:33 a.m. He became known as a phantom, a malevolent force that could not be stopped, leaving death in his wake.

As the years passed, Nathaniel's hatred consumed him. He no longer sought just revenge against the Marstons but against the entire town. He blamed them all for his family's downfall, for the loss of his father, and for the years of ridicule and rejection he had endured. In his twisted mind, every resident of Whispers Creek was complicit in the crimes against his family, and they all deserved to suffer.

But his greatest revenge was yet to come. Nathaniel discovered that his time-traveling abilities were not without consequence. The more he manipulated time, the more he began to lose his own sense of it. His memories of his original life began to fade, replaced by a singular focus on his mission of vengeance. He became trapped in a loop of his own making, a shadow of the man he once was, cursed to roam the corridors of time, forever seeking retribution.

Now, with Ivy on his trail, Nathaniel's wrath is once again unleashed upon Whispers Creek. But this time, his connection to the town is even deeper, as Ivy represents the final link to the town's dark past—a past Nathaniel is determined to erase, no matter the cost.

Chapter 5: *A Race Against Time*

The weight of Nathaniel Grayson's tragic history pressed heavily on Ivy's mind as she left Mrs. Thatcher's crumbling mansion. The revelation about Grayson's vendetta against Whispers Creek and his ability to travel through time had shaken her to her core. But Ivy knew she had no time to dwell on fear. Every second counted—if she didn't act fast, Lily might never be found, and more lives could be lost.

Determined to uncover more about Grayson's dark legacy, Ivy went where it all began: the Grayson mansion. The once-grand estate, now a decrepit ruin on the outskirts of town, was said to be cursed, abandoned for decades after Nathaniel's disappearance. The townspeople spoke of strange occurrences at the mansion—flickering lights, eerie sounds, and ghostly apparitions. Ivy had always dismissed these stories as mere legends, but now she knew there was something far more sinister at play.

With her heart pounding, Ivy made her way through the thick fog that shrouded the mansion. The air was cold and damp, and the wind whispered through the trees, carrying the faint echoes of a forgotten past. The mansion loomed before her, its once-majestic columns now cracked and weathered, its windows shattered, and its doors hanging off their hinges. Ivy steeled herself and stepped inside.

The interior of the mansion was even more decayed than she had imagined. Dust coated every surface, and cobwebs hung like ghostly curtains from the ceiling. The air was thick with the scent of mold and decay, but beneath it, Ivy could sense something else—a lingering presence, as if the house itself was alive, watching her every move.

As she explored the mansion, Ivy discovered that the house had been left almost exactly as it had been the day Nathaniel disappeared. His laboratory, the epicenter of his experiments, was hidden in the basement, accessible only through a secret passageway Ivy found behind an old bookcase in the study. The passage was narrow and winding, its walls lined with shelves filled with books, journals, and strange mechanical devices. It was clear that Nathaniel had been a man of extraordinary intellect and ambition, but also of deep obsession.

In the laboratory, Ivy found a treasure trove of clues. Nathaniel's journals, filled with complex equations, diagrams, and detailed notes about his experiments with time, were scattered across a large wooden desk. The journal entries were written in a feverish hand, with pages upon pages dedicated to his theories on time travel and the manipulation of temporal dimensions.

Ivy pored over the journals, piecing together Nathaniel's descent into madness. He had become obsessed with the idea of controlling time, not just to reverse his father's illness but to exact revenge on those who had wronged him. He believed that by creating a device capable of manipulating time—a pocket watch with the power to open doorways between different eras—he could rewrite history itself.

One of the journals contained a blueprint for the pocket watch, detailing how it was constructed using a combination of advanced mechanics and arcane rituals. The watch was more than just a machine—it was a conduit for dark, ancient forces that Nathaniel had summoned during his experiments. He had bound these forces to the watch, imbuing it with the power to bend time to his will. But in doing so, Nathaniel had unwittingly tethered his own soul to the device, becoming a slave to the very power he had sought to control.

The more Ivy read, the more she realized that Nathaniel's vendetta wasn't just about revenge. He had come to see himself as a guardian of time, a force that could punish those who disrupted the natural order. In his twisted mind, he was a judge, jury, and executioner, erasing those he deemed unworthy from the timeline. And now, with the watch in Ivy's possession, she was the only one who could stop him.

But Ivy also found something unexpected in the journals—glimpses of the man Nathaniel had once been. Buried beneath the layers of anger and madness were entries that spoke of a deep love for his family, a longing for acceptance, and a desire to use his knowledge for good. He had once dreamed of becoming a great scientist, of using his discoveries to help others. But the cruelty of the world had twisted those dreams into a nightmare.

As Ivy delved deeper into Nathaniel's writings, she uncovered a clue that might hold the key to stopping him. Nathaniel had written about a "Time Anchor"—a fixed point in time that he had created as a failsafe, a place where he could return to if his experiments went wrong. The Anchor was connected to the pocket watch, serving as a reset point for the timeline. If Ivy could find the Anchor, she might be able to sever Nathaniel's connection to the watch, trapping him in one time period and ending his reign of terror.

The problem was, Nathaniel had deliberately obscured the location of the Time Anchor, encrypting it in a complex code that only someone with a deep understanding of his work could decipher. Ivy knew she didn't have much time. She needed help, but she couldn't trust anyone in this strange, old version of Whispers Creek.

With the journal in hand, Ivy returned to Mrs. Thatcher, who, despite her fear, agreed to help Ivy decode the encrypted messages. They worked together for hours, poring over the notes and equations, trying to piece together the puzzle that Nathaniel had left behind.

As they worked, Ivy began to notice strange things happening around her—time seemed to warp and bend, with objects moving out of place and shadows flickering in the corners of her vision. She knew that Nathaniel was close, watching her, trying to manipulate the timeline to stop her. But Ivy was determined not to let him win.

Finally, after what felt like days, Ivy and Mrs. Thatcher cracked the code. The Time Anchor was hidden in the town's clock tower, the very symbol of Whispers Creek's existence. The clock tower, once a beacon of hope and progress for the town, had become the epicenter of Nathaniel's dark power.

With this knowledge, Ivy knew she was running out of time—literally. Nathaniel would soon realize what she had discovered, and he would stop at nothing to prevent her from reaching the clock tower. But Ivy was ready. She had the pocket watch, the knowledge of Nathaniel's past, and a determination fueled by her love for Lily and the desire to save her town.

As Ivy left Mrs. Thatcher's home and headed for the clock tower, she knew that this would be her final confrontation with Nathaniel Grayson. The race against time had begun, and she was the only one who could stop the cycle of death that had plagued Whispers Creek for over a century.

Chapter 6: *The Final Hour*

Ivy stepped out of Mrs. Thatcher's house, clutching the pocket watch and the decoded journal entries. The night was eerily quiet, with the full moon casting an otherworldly glow over Whispers Creek. The town seemed frozen in time, as if the very air held its breath, waiting for what was to come. Ivy's heart pounded in her chest, each beat reminding her of the precious minutes slipping away. She knew she was racing not just against the clock but against Nathaniel Grayson himself.

The clock tower loomed in the distance, its silhouette stark against the night sky. Ivy knew it was more than just a structure; it was the very heart of Nathaniel's power, the Time Anchor that connected him to the pocket watch and allowed him to manipulate time. If she could sever that connection, she could trap Nathaniel in a single era, ending his reign of terror once and for all.

As she made her way through the darkened streets, Ivy couldn't shake the feeling that she was being watched. The shadows seemed to move with her, whispering her name in voices that weren't quite human. The town, once familiar, now felt like a maze of shifting realities, each step threatening to pull her into another time, another place. But Ivy forced herself to focus. She had to stay in the present—there was no room for fear or doubt now.

The closer she got to the clock tower, the more the air around her seemed to thicken, as if time itself was warping, resisting her approach. Ivy's mind raced, replaying everything she had learned about Nathaniel, his experiments, and the Time Anchor. She knew that destroying the Anchor wouldn't be as simple as smashing a clock or cutting a wire. It was tied to something deeper, something that had been rooted in the town's history for over a century.

When she finally reached the base of the clock tower, Ivy hesitated for a moment, looking up at the towering structure. The clock face, with its ornate hands, was frozen at 3:33 a.m.—the Silent Hour, the time when Nathaniel always struck. The tower itself was ancient, its stone walls worn and cracked, yet it emanated a sense of power, a connection to something far greater than the town itself.

Ivy steeled herself and entered the tower. The interior was dark and musty, filled with the scent of old wood and rusted metal. The only light came from the moon filtering through the broken windows, casting long, jagged shadows across the floor. Ivy's footsteps echoed as she ascended the narrow staircase, each creak of the wood sounding like a gunshot in the silence.

As she climbed higher, Ivy began to notice strange symbols etched into the walls—symbols she recognized from Nathaniel's journal. They were the same symbols he had used to bind the dark forces to the pocket watch, to create the Time Anchor. The air grew colder, and Ivy felt a tingling sensation in her fingers, as if the very fabric of time was unraveling around her.

Finally, she reached the top of the tower, where the massive clock mechanism was housed. The gears, once a marvel of engineering, were now covered in dust and grime, their intricate workings frozen in place. But Ivy knew the true danger wasn't in the gears—it was in the heart of the clock itself, where the Time Anchor was hidden.

Nathaniel's journal had mentioned a chamber within the clock, accessible only by those who knew the secret. Ivy scanned the room, searching for anything that might resemble an entrance. Her eyes fell on a small, ornate keyhole embedded in the base of the clock. She knelt down, pulling the pocket watch from her coat pocket, and noticed something she hadn't seen before—a small, hidden compartment in the back of the watch. With trembling fingers, she opened it to reveal a tiny, intricately carved key.

Ivy inserted the key into the keyhole, and with a click, a hidden panel slid open, revealing a narrow passageway that led deep into the heart of the clock. Taking a deep breath, Ivy entered the passage, her footsteps echoing on the stone floor.

The passage led to a small, circular chamber, dimly lit by the pale light filtering through cracks in the walls. In the center of the room stood an ancient, weathered pedestal, upon which rested a strange, glowing orb—the Time Anchor. The orb pulsed with a sickly, greenish light, its surface swirling with dark, chaotic energy. Ivy could feel the immense power emanating from it, a power that was both ancient and malevolent.

She approached the pedestal cautiously, knowing that this was the source of Nathaniel's power, the very thing that allowed him to traverse time and leave his deadly mark on Whispers Creek. But as she reached out to touch the orb, a sudden, icy wind swept through the chamber, and the room darkened. Ivy's heart raced as she heard a familiar voice echoing through the chamber.

"You're too late, Ivy," Nathaniel's voice whispered, cold and menacing. *"You think you can stop me? You think you can change the past? Time is my domain, and I am its master."*

Ivy spun around, but there was no one there—only shadows that seemed to move and twist of their own accord. The temperature in the chamber plummeted, and Ivy could see her breath in the air. She knew Nathaniel was close, manipulating time itself to stop her. But she couldn't let him win. She couldn't let Lily's fate be sealed by a madman from another time.

Steeling herself against the cold and the fear, Ivy turned back to the orb. She remembered what Nathaniel had written in his journal about the nature of the Time Anchor—it was not just a physical object but a convergence point for all the timelines Nathaniel had manipulated. To destroy it, Ivy would need to sever the connections between the timelines, to break the loop that Nathaniel had created.

Drawing on everything she had learned from Mrs. Thatcher and Nathaniel's journals, Ivy focused on the orb, channeling her willpower into the task at hand. She visualized the different timelines, the strands of time that Nathaniel had twisted and bent to his will. In her mind's eye, she saw the threads of time, all leading back to this one point—the Time Anchor.

With a surge of determination, Ivy reached out and placed her hands on the orb. The moment her fingers touched the surface, a shock of energy coursed through her, as if the very essence of time itself was trying to repel her. But Ivy held on, her grip tightening as she concentrated on unraveling the connections.

The orb began to pulse faster, its light growing brighter and more erratic. The chamber shook, and the shadows around Ivy writhed in agony, but she refused to let go. She could feel the timelines tugging at her, pulling her in different directions, but she focused on the present—on this moment, this place. She thought of Lily, of Mrs. Thatcher, of the town that had suffered for so long under Nathaniel's curse. She thought of the future she wanted to save, the lives she needed to protect.

With a final burst of strength, Ivy channeled all her energy into the orb, severing the connections between the timelines, and breaking the cycle that had allowed Nathaniel to exist outside of time. The orb glowed brighter, and then, with a deafening crack, it shattered into a thousand pieces, the dark energy within it dissipating into the air like smoke.

The moment the orb shattered; the chamber was engulfed in blinding light. Ivy felt herself being pulled in all directions at once as if the very fabric of time was unraveling around her. But she held on, focusing on the present, on the now. The light grew brighter and brighter until it consumed everything, and then, with a sudden jolt, it was gone.

Epilogue: *The Watcher*

With Nathaniel defeated Ivy returned to her own time, exhausted but triumphant. Whispers Creek began to heal, the weight of its dark history lifting at last. But Ivy knew that time was a fragile thing, and the secrets of the past were never truly buried.

As she tucked the pocket watch away, she couldn't shake the feeling that someone—or something—was still watching her. The watch's hands were still, but in the silence, Ivy could almost hear the faintest ticking.

The Silent Hour, it seemed, was far from over.

Book II

Chronicles of the Silent Hour: Return of the Watcher

Chapter 1: *The Uneasy Return*

Ivy Whitlock stood at the edge of the woods; the pocket watch clutched tightly in her hand. She had narrowly escaped the clutches of Nathaniel Grayson, trapping him in a time loop and seemingly putting an end to his reign of terror. As she turned the hands of the watch to the present day, she felt the familiar whirl of colors and lights envelop her, transporting her through the fabric of time.

The world slowly came back into focus, and Ivy found herself standing in the very spot where she had first discovered the watch. The sun was just beginning to rise, casting a warm glow over Whispers Creek. For a moment, Ivy felt an immense relief wash over her—she was home.

But as she walked through the streets of her hometown, Ivy realized that returning home would not be as simple as she had imagined. The town looked the same, yet she felt different. The people who greeted her with smiles and friendly waves seemed distant, as if they could sense the burden of her experiences. She couldn't shake the feeling that she was a stranger in her own life.

The next few weeks were a blur of attempts to resume normalcy. Ivy went back to school, spent time with her parents, and visited familiar places, but everything felt surreal. She couldn't share her experiences with anyone, not even her closest friends, for fear of putting them in danger of being dismissed as crazy. The weight of her secret was heavy, and it left her feeling isolated.

One afternoon, in search of a distraction, Ivy decided to explore her attic. It was a space she had rarely ventured into, filled with old family belongings and memories of the past. As she sifted through boxes of dusty photographs and faded letters, she hoped to find something that would ground her, remind her of who she was before her life was turned upside down.

While rummaging through the clutter, Ivy stumbled upon a trunk that had belonged to her grandmother, Margaret Whitlock. It was locked, but Ivy found the key hidden beneath a stack of quilts. As she opened the trunk, the scent of aged paper filled the air. Inside, she found a collection of her grandmother's old journals, chronicling her life in Whispers Creek.

Curious, Ivy began to read. Her grandmother's words painted a vivid picture of the town's history, its secrets, and the challenges the family had faced over the years. But it was one journal in particular that caught her attention. It was dated shortly after Nathaniel Grayson's first murder and described a series of dreams her grandmother had experienced—dreams of a young woman fighting to stop a killer across different eras. The descriptions were uncannily similar to Ivy's own journey.

As Ivy read on, she felt a strange connection to her grandmother, a sense that they were part of something larger than themselves. It was as if Margaret had known that Ivy would one day face the same darkness and had left these journals as a guide. The more Ivy read, the more she understood that her family was deeply entwined with the mysteries of Whispers Creek and the Silent Hour.

The discovery of her grandmother's journals gave Ivy a renewed sense of purpose. She realized that settling back into her old life would require more than just blending in; it would require embracing her role as the Watcher and protecting the town from the shadows of the past. With this new resolve, Ivy set out to uncover the secrets of her family's legacy and the true nature of the Silent Hour.

Chapter 2: *Reclaiming the Past*

Determined to delve deeper into the mystery of the Silent Hour, Ivy sought out Mrs. Thatcher once again. The local historian had been an invaluable resource during Ivy's previous adventure, and Ivy knew that Mrs. Thatcher's extensive knowledge of Whispers Creek's history could provide crucial insights into her family's legacy.

Mrs. Thatcher greeted Ivy with a knowing smile as she entered the historian's cozy, cluttered home. The shelves were lined with old books, town records, and various artifacts that Mrs. Thatcher had collected over the years. It was a treasure trove of history, and Ivy felt a sense of anticipation as she stepped inside.

"Ivy, my dear, I've been expecting you," Mrs. Thatcher said, her eyes twinkling with curiosity. "I had a feeling that you'd be back to uncover more of the town's secrets."

Ivy nodded, feeling a mix of excitement and apprehension. "I found my grandmother's journals in the attic," she began. "They mention the Silent Hour and describe dreams that are eerily similar to what I experienced. I think my family has been connected to this phenomenon for generations."

Mrs. Thatcher's expression turned serious. "The Silent Hour is an ancient and powerful force, Ivy. It's been a part of Whispers Creek for as long as anyone can remember. But much of its history has been lost or forgotten."

The two of them settled down at Mrs. Thatcher's large oak table, which was already strewn with old maps and documents. Mrs. Thatcher pulled out a leather-bound book from one of the shelves and placed it in front of Ivy. The cover was embossed with a symbol that Ivy recognized from her grandmother's journals—a circle with intricate patterns radiating from the center.

"This is one of the few surviving records of the original coven that protected Whispers Creek," Mrs. Thatcher explained. "The coven was composed of wise women and men who understood the power of the Silent Hour and used it to safeguard the town from various threats."

Ivy's eyes widened as she flipped through the pages. The book contained detailed descriptions of rituals, spells, and incantations that the coven had used to harness the power of the Silent Hour. There were also accounts of their battles against dark forces that had threatened the town over the centuries.

"What happened to the coven?" Ivy asked, her voice filled with wonder.

Mrs. Thatcher sighed. "Over time, as the town grew and modernized, the coven's knowledge was dismissed as mere superstition. Many of the records were lost or destroyed, and the coven eventually disbanded. But the power of the Silent Hour remained, and those who sought to misuse it, like Nathaniel Grayson, have caused great harm."

As they continued to explore the book, Ivy discovered a passage that mentioned a prophecy about a "Watcher"—a guardian destined to protect the balance of time and ensure that the Silent Hour was not corrupted. The prophecy was vague, but it hinted at a great responsibility and power that would be passed down through generations.

"I think this is about you, Ivy," Mrs. Thatcher said softly. "You are the Watcher, the one who can reclaim the lost knowledge and protect our town from the darkness that lurks in the shadows."

Ivy felt a mixture of pride and trepidation. The idea of being the Watcher was daunting, but it also felt right. Her family's legacy and the coven's wisdom were now in her hands, and she was determined to use them for good.

Together, Ivy and Mrs. Thatcher began the painstaking process of piecing together the coven's lost knowledge. They spent hours deciphering the rituals and studying the symbols, working to understand the true nature of the Silent Hour and how to control it. Mrs. Thatcher taught Ivy about the importance of balance and respect for the natural order, emphasizing that the Silent Hour was not just a tool but a living force that required careful stewardship.

As Ivy immersed herself in this ancient wisdom, she felt a growing connection to her ancestors and a deeper understanding of her role as the Watcher. She knew that the journey ahead would be challenging, but with Mrs. Thatcher's guidance and her grandmother's journals as a guide, she was ready to face whatever the future might hold.

Chapter 3: *The Coven Reborn*

As Ivy delved deeper into the mysteries of the Silent Hour, she realized she couldn't shoulder the burden of protecting Whispers Creek alone. The knowledge she had gained from her grandmother's journals and Mrs. Thatcher's guidance was invaluable, but she needed allies—people who understood the stakes and were willing to fight for the town's future. Ivy decided to rebuild the coven with a modern twist, one that could adapt to the challenges of their era.

She began by reaching out to her closest friends: Claire, a talented artist/botanist with an intuitive sense for the mystical; and Noah, a tech-savvy teenager with a knack for uncovering secrets. They had been by Ivy's side through thick and thin, and she knew she could trust them with the town's greatest secret.

Ivy invited them to her home, where she revealed everything, she had learned about the Silent Hour and her family's legacy as Watchers. As she spoke, she watched their reactions carefully, unsure of how they would respond to the weight of her revelation.

Claire was the first to speak, her eyes wide with a mix of awe and excitement. "Ivy, this is incredible. It's like we're part of a real-life fantasy story!"

Noah, ever the skeptic, raised an eyebrow but couldn't hide his curiosity. "So, you're telling us that time travel and magic are real? And we're supposed to help protect the town from some ancient evil?"

With her friends on board, Ivy felt a surge of confidence. They spent the next few weeks learning everything they could about the original coven's rituals and spells. Mrs. Thatcher provided them with more books and artifacts, and together, they worked to decipher the ancient texts and adapt the practices for their modern-day coven.

As the group grew closer, they became more attuned to the rhythms of the Silent Hour. They began to sense disturbances in the town, small anomalies that hinted at a greater problem. It was during one of their training sessions that Claire noticed something strange—a pattern of symbols appearing in the woods near the old mill.

The symbols matched those in Ivy's grandmother's journals, indicating a hidden message or warning. As they investigated further, they discovered that the symbols formed a path leading deeper into the forest. As they followed the path of symbols it led to a rock wall. Noah said out of breath "This is a Dead End." Ivy looked around her and saw something on a nearby tree as she got closer, she realized it was a *Murderer Mark*. Noah sat down on a rock to rest and the mark started to glow and revealed a hole in the wall. Noah looked at it and shouted, "Looks like a keyhole." Ivy ran over to get a look she said "A pocket watch goes here." So, she took out the watch from her pants pocket and placed it in the hole then the ground opened next to the mark.

They all went down the steps that were in the ground opening they found an abandoned cabin, and inside, they stumbled upon Lily.

Lily was disoriented and frightened, her memories of the past few weeks a jumbled blur. She spoke of a dark figure who had lured her into the woods and kept her captive. The figure had been searching for something, asking Lily about the Silent Hour and the coven's secrets.

Realizing the urgency of the situation, Ivy and her friends brought Lily back to town and alerted her family. The town was abuzz with relief at Lily's safe return, but Ivy couldn't shake the feeling that their troubles were far from over. The discovery of the symbols and Lily's abduction confirmed that a new threat was looming over Whispers Creek.

Chapter 4: *A New Coven*

With Lily safely back in town, Ivy and her friends knew that their work was far from over. The discovery of Lily in the abandoned cabin had not only validated their fears about a new threat but also highlighted the importance of their mission. The coven was more determined than ever to protect Whispers Creek and uncover the truth behind the recent disturbances.

Lily's recovery was swift but emotional. She was deeply shaken by her ordeal but was grateful to be home. The initial confusion and fear slowly gave way to a sense of relief as she reunited with her family. Ivy visited her regularly, offering support and reassurance as Lily began to piece together the fragments of her memory.

During one of these visits, Lily opened up about her experience. She recounted how she had been lured into the woods by a dark figure who seemed to know a great deal about the Silent Hour. The figure had been insistent, demanding to know about the coven and the secrets it protected. When Lily had been unable to provide the information, the figure had become threatening, leaving her in a state of fear.

Ivy listened carefully, her heart aching for her friend. The dark figure's actions confirmed that their adversary was growing bolder and more dangerous. As Lily recounted the details, Ivy knew that they needed to act quickly to prevent further threats.

Seeing Lily's bravery and resolve, Ivy felt compelled to ask her if she would join the newly formed coven. It was a significant decision, one that would involve her in the heart of their efforts to safeguard the town.

"Lily, I know you've been through so much, but we need your help," Ivy said gently. "The coven needs all the strength and courage we can get. We've already seen how dangerous this threat can be. Will you join us?"

Lily looked at Ivy with a mixture of determination and apprehension. "I want to help. I've seen firsthand how real the danger is, and I don't want anyone else to go through what I did. I'll join you."

The coven welcomed Lily with open arms. Her addition brought a new sense of unity and strength to their group. As they gathered in the woods, under the ancient trees that had witnessed countless generations, they held a formal induction ceremony for Lily.

With her friends and the guidance of Mrs. Thatcher, Lily quickly adapted to the coven's rituals and training. Her experiences made her a valuable member, and her intuitive sense of danger proved to be a crucial asset. She had a deep understanding of the threats they faced, and her courage inspired the rest of the team.

The coven, now complete with Lily's addition, redoubled their efforts to protect Whispers Creek. They conducted regular meetings to discuss their findings and strategies. Claire's artistic skills produced new protective charms and symbols, Noah's tech solutions kept them connected and alert, Alex's scientific analysis helped them understand the anomalies, and Lily's firsthand experience provided crucial insights into the enemy's tactics.

Their teamwork paid off as they began to detect subtle shifts in the town's energy. The symbols Lily had seen in the woods were appearing in other locations, suggesting that their adversary was marking areas for a future attack.

One evening, as the sun set and the moon rose high in the sky, the coven gathered at their meeting spot in the woods. They performed a ritual to strengthen their bonds and enhance their protective spells. The energy in the air was palpable, a testament to their growing power and unity.

As Ivy looked around at her friends, now more like family, she felt a deep sense of pride and hope. The coven had come together to face the challenges ahead, and with Lily's strength and resolve added to their ranks, they were ready to confront the darkness that threatened their town.

Together, they would stand against whatever came their way, united by their purpose and the unbreakable bond of their shared mission. The

Silent Hour was a force to be reckoned with, but with their newfound strength, Ivy and her coven were determined to protect Whispers Creek and ensure its safety for generations to come.

Chapter 5: *The Battle for Time*

As the Timekeepers worked to uncover the identity of their new adversary, Ivy discovered that the pocket watch held more secrets than she had imagined. It was a key, capable of unlocking portals to different eras and dimensions. But with such power came great responsibility.

The Timekeepers' investigation led them to a forgotten part of town, where they found a hidden laboratory. Inside, they discovered plans for a device that could control the Silent Hour and bend time to its wielder's will. The blueprints were signed by none other than Nathaniel Grayson.

Before they could destroy the plans, they were confronted by a shadowy figure—

The coven's vigilance paid off when they discovered that the symbols were more than just random markings. Each symbol corresponded to a location tied to the history of the Silent Hour, suggesting that their adversary was methodically preparing for something significant. The symbols also revealed a pattern—a convergence point where the energies of the Silent Hour would be the strongest.

Noah's tech analysis revealed that the disturbances were not just localized but were creating fluctuations in the town's energy field. He found that the patterns aligned with an old, hidden network of tunnels beneath Whispers Creek, which had been part of the original coven's protective measures. The tunnels, long forgotten by most, were rumored to contain powerful artifacts and knowledge related to the Silent Hour.

The coven decided to explore the tunnels to uncover any clues about the dark figure's plans and to secure any potential threats. They set out on a crisp autumn evening, armed with their knowledge of the Silent Hour and their newly crafted protective charms.

Entering the tunnels was like stepping into another world. The air was damp and filled with the musty scent of earth. The walls were lined with ancient symbols and faded murals depicting scenes of battles between the coven and dark forces.

As they ventured deeper, they encountered a series of traps and obstacles, remnants of the coven's original protective measures. Alex's scientific expertise and Noah's tech skills proved invaluable as they navigated these dangers. Alex's knowledge of mechanics helped them disarm traps, while Noah used his gadgets to detect hidden passages and traps.

The deeper they went, the more the atmosphere grew tense. The tunnels seemed to close in on them, and Ivy felt a palpable sense of foreboding. It was as if the darkness of the past was seeping into the present, echoing the threats they faced.

Eventually, they reached a large, dimly lit chamber. At its center stood an altar covered in ancient relics and manuscripts. In the corner of the chamber, they found a dusty, old chest that seemed to radiate an ominous energy. Ivy recognized the symbols on the chest from her grandmother's journals—they were symbols of binding and containment.

As they approached the chest, the temperature in the chamber dropped. A dark figure materialized before them, shrouded in shadows and emanating a chilling presence. It was clear that this figure was not only aware of their presence but had been expecting them.

The dark figure's voice was low and menacing. "You're too late. The power of the Silent Hour will soon be mine to control, and there's nothing you can do to stop it."

A fierce battle ensued. The coven fought with all their might, using their knowledge of the Silent Hour and their protective charms. Claire's artistic creations came to life, forming barriers and wards that pushed back the dark figure. Noah's gadgets provided critical support, illuminating the chamber and detecting weak points in the figure's defenses. Alex's scientific knowledge helped them understand the nature of the figure's powers and how to counter them.

The battle reached its climax when Ivy, wielding the pocket watch, confronted the dark figure directly. The watch's power was immense, but it required careful control. Ivy focused all her energy on the watch, channeling its power to weaken the dark figure and disrupt its control over the chamber's energy.

With a final surge of strength, Ivy activated the watch's protective spell, creating a barrier that trapped the dark figure within a time loop. The figure's form twisted and contorted as it was pulled into the loop, rendering it powerless and unable to escape.

The chamber fell silent as the battle ended. Exhausted but victorious, the coven regrouped and examined the chest. Inside, they found a collection of powerful artifacts and manuscripts that detailed the history of the Silent Hour and its many guardians. These artifacts, if used wisely, could provide valuable insights and aid in their continued protection of Whispers Creek.

Chapter 6: *Restoring Balance*

Emerging from the tunnels as dawn broke, the coven felt a profound sense of accomplishment. They had confronted the darkness and emerged victorious, but they knew their work was far from over. The Silent Hour was a powerful force, and there would always be those who sought to misuse its power.

With the dark figure defeated and the artifacts secured, Ivy and her friends returned to their normal lives, but with a renewed sense of purpose. The coven continued to meet regularly, studying the newly discovered artifacts and preparing for any future threats.

As the town of Whispers Creek returned to its peaceful routine, Ivy looked out over the familiar landscape with a sense of hope. The battles they had fought and won had forged a strong bond among the coven members, and they were ready to face whatever challenges lay ahead.

Together, they had proven that the Silent Hour could be protected, and that with courage and unity, they could overcome even the darkest threats. The future of Whispers Creek was in their hands, and they were prepared to safeguard it with all their might.

With the immediate threat neutralized, Ivy and the Timekeepers set about restoring the balance of time in Whispers Creek. They sealed the laboratory and safeguarded the coven's knowledge, ensuring it wouldn't fall into the wrong hands again.

Ivy felt a deep sense of fulfillment as she watched her town slowly return to normal. The Silent Hour, once a source of fear and danger, had become a part of her identity—a reminder of her role as the Watcher.

As the seasons changed and life went on, Ivy knew that the peace she had fought for was fragile. The secrets of the Silent Hour were still out there, waiting to be discovered. But for now, Whispers Creek was safe, and Ivy was ready to face whatever the future might hold.

Epilogue: *The Keeper of Time*

Years later, Ivy stood at the edge of the woods, the pocket watch in her hand. She had learned to harness its power, using it to protect her town and the people she loved. The Silent Hour had become her ally, a constant companion in her journey through time.

As she watched the sun set over Whispers Creek, Ivy knew that her story was just beginning. The chronicles of the Silent Hour were far from over, and she was ready to face whatever challenges lay ahead, as the Keeper of Time.

Book III

43

Chronicles of the Silent Hour: Shadows of Betrayal

Chapter 1: *The Keepers of Time*

The early morning mist hung low over Whispers Creek as the newly formed coven gathered at the heart of the woods, the forest's tall, ancient trees standing as silent witnesses to their solemn ceremony. Ivy and her companions stood in a circle, the chill in the air reminding them of the weight of their new responsibilities. As the first light of dawn filtered through the branches, Ivy's thoughts turned to the challenge of their new roles as the Keepers of Time.

With the dissolution of the dark force and the binding of the coven, the Silent Hour had revealed its true purpose. The coven was no longer merely a gathering of like-minded individuals; they were the guardians of a powerful and enigmatic force that held the threads of time itself. Their duty was to ensure the balance and integrity of time, to safeguard it from those who would seek to misuse it for personal gain or malevolent intent.

Mrs. Thatcher, now the coven's elder advisor, had spent the past weeks teaching them the intricacies of their new roles. The Silent Hour, she explained, was a delicate phenomenon that allowed for the convergence of past, present, and future, but it was not without its dangers. History was riddled with instances of those who had tried to manipulate it, and the coven had to be ever vigilant.

"Ivy, you must lead with both wisdom and caution," Mrs. Thatcher had warned. "The Silent Hour's power is as much a responsibility as it is a gift. You must guide the coven in protecting it."

The Keepers of Time quickly learned that their duties went beyond their traditional rituals and spells. They found themselves facing new challenges, such as deciphering cryptic messages left by past covens and monitoring the subtle shifts in the fabric of time. These shifts, often caused by the misuse of the Silent Hour's power, could have far-reaching consequences, altering the course of history or impacting the future in unforeseen ways.

As they worked together, tensions occasionally flared within the coven. The enormity of their task and the fear of making a misstep weighed heavily on them. Ivy, as the leader, struggled with the responsibility of guiding her friends while also ensuring their safety. She knew that one wrong move could have disastrous consequences, not just for them but for all of Whispers Creek.

Lily, too, was finding her footing again. After her harrowing experience with the dark force, she was more determined than ever to support Ivy and the coven. However, the lingering effects of her ordeal sometimes made it difficult for her to fully trust her own instincts.

Despite the challenges, the coven's bond grew stronger. Each member brought their unique skills and perspectives to the group, creating a well-rounded team capable of facing whatever threats the Silent Hour might attract. They trained together, honed their abilities, and studied the ancient texts that held the secrets of time.

As the sun rose higher in the sky, casting warm light over the clearing, Ivy looked around at her friends. She felt a surge of pride and gratitude for their dedication and courage. They had come so far, and she knew that together, they could overcome any obstacle.

"We are the Keepers of Time," Ivy declared, her voice ringing with conviction. "We will protect the Silent Hour and the legacy of our ancestors. No matter what comes our way, we will stand together."

The coven members nodded in agreement; their resolve clear. With the dawn of a new day, they were ready to face the unknown, united in their purpose and bound by their shared destiny. The Silent Hour awaited them, and the coven was prepared to meet its challenges head-on.

Chapter 2: *The Gathering Storm*

Ivy couldn't shake the feeling that something was wrong. It was subtle at first—a sense of unease that lingered in the corners of her mind. The newly reformed coven had been making strides, strengthening their bond and refining their skills. Yet, despite their successes, a shadow seemed to be creeping over Whispers Creek.

As the Keepers of Time, the coven was acutely attuned to the rhythms of the town and its hidden energies. Ivy noticed that the usual vibrancy of Whispers Creek had dulled. People were quieter, their laughter less frequent. Even the creek itself, which normally babbled cheerfully, seemed subdued, as if the water sensed the tension in the air.

Ivy's concerns were compounded by her observations of Lily, her best friend and confidante. Lily's usual bright demeanor had been replaced by an uncharacteristic solemnity. She was often lost in thought, her eyes reflecting a storm of emotions. Ivy could tell that something was weighing heavily on her friend, and she was determined to find out what it was.

One evening, as the coven gathered for their weekly meeting in the woods, Ivy decided to address the group. They sat in a circle around a small fire, its flickering flames casting dancing shadows on their faces.

"I've been feeling uneasy lately," Ivy began, her gaze meeting each of her friends in turn. "There's something happening in Whispers Creek, something we can't see but can definitely feel. We need to be on alert."

Noah, the analyst, nodded in agreement. "I've noticed some unusual data patterns," he said, pulling out his tablet. "There are fluctuations in the town's energy levels, spikes that don't correspond to any natural phenomena."

Claire, the herbalist, leaned forward. "And the plants in my garden are behaving strangely. They're wilting despite the care I give them, and the birds seem restless."

Mrs. Thatcher, the coven's elder advisor, listened intently. Her eyes, wise with the knowledge of years, were filled with concern. "These signs cannot be ignored," she said gravely. "We must prepare ourselves for whatever is to come."

With the group's agreement, Ivy outlined a plan to increase their vigilance. They would take shifts monitoring the town and the woods, keeping an eye out for any unusual activity. Noah would continue his analysis, searching for any patterns or anomalies that might provide a clue. Claire would work on strengthening their protective spells, drawing on her deep knowledge of herbs and nature.

Lily, who had been quiet throughout the discussion, finally spoke up. "I think we should also consider the possibility of someone—or something—trying to disrupt the Silent Hour," she suggested. Her voice was steady, but Ivy could hear the underlying tension.

Ivy nodded, her resolve hardening. "You're right, Lily. We can't rule anything out. We need to be ready for anything."

As the meeting drew to a close, Ivy felt a renewed sense of purpose. They had faced challenges before, and they would face them again. The coven was strong, their bond unbreakable. Whatever was lurking in the shadows of Whispers Creek, they would confront it together.

The night air was cool as the coven members dispersed, each heading home with a heightened sense of awareness. Ivy and Lily walked together, the moonlight guiding their steps. As they parted ways, Ivy placed a reassuring hand on Lily's shoulder. "We'll get through this, Lily. Together."

Lily smiled, but there was a hint of sadness in her eyes. "I know, Ivy. I trust you."

As Ivy watched her friend disappear into the night, she couldn't help but feel a pang of worry. The gathering storm was closer than ever, and she knew they had to be ready for whatever it might bring.

Chapter 3: *Echoes of the Past*

The air in Ivy's attic room was thick with dust and the scent of aged paper. She had spent countless hours here since becoming the leader of the coven, poring over her grandmother's journals and other ancient texts in search of guidance. Each entry, each faded page, held fragments of wisdom from the past, pieces of a puzzle that she was desperately trying to put together.

But today, as she leafed through a particularly worn journal, something caught her eye—a passage that sent a shiver down her spine. It spoke of a force, dark and malevolent, that once threatened Whispers Creek, a force that seemed eerily similar to the unsettling presence Ivy had been sensing.

The journal entry was dated over a century ago, written in her great-grandmother's careful script. It described a time when the coven had faced a grave danger—a dark force that had seeped into the town, feeding off the fears and negative emotions of its inhabitants. The force had been elusive, hiding in shadows, corrupting the weak-minded and those who had lost hope.

Ivy's eyes scanned the words, her heart pounding in her chest. The descriptions were vague, as if her great-grandmother had been too afraid to put the full extent of the horror into words. But the warning was clear: this force could not be allowed to take hold, for once it did, it would spread like a plague, devouring everything in its path.

The journal went on to describe how the coven of that time had managed to drive the force back, sealing it away with powerful magic. But the seal was not permanent. It required vigilance, constant reinforcement, and the unity of the coven to keep the darkness at bay.

As Ivy read on, a terrible realization dawned on her. The symptoms her great-grandmother had described—the strange behavior of the townspeople, the withering of plants, the unease in the air—matched exactly what Ivy and the coven had been experiencing.

Could it be that the dark force had returned, drawn back to Whispers Creek after all these years? And if so, was the coven strong enough to stop it this time?

Ivy's mind raced as she considered the implications. The seal that had been placed so long ago must have weakened over the years. Perhaps it had even been broken. The coven's rituals, meant to protect the town, might not be enough to hold back something so ancient and powerful.

She thought of Lily, who had been acting so strangely. Could the darkness have already found a foothold in her? The idea made Ivy's stomach turn. She knew she had to act quickly, but she couldn't do it alone.

Ivy wasted no time. She gathered the journals and headed straight to Mrs. Thatcher's home. The historian's house was a sanctuary of sorts, filled with relics and books that told the story of Whispers Creek's long and complicated history. It was the perfect place to seek answers.

Mrs. Thatcher greeted Ivy with a knowing look, as if she had been expecting her. "You've found something, haven't you?" she asked, leading Ivy into a cozy sitting room where a fire crackled warmly in the hearth.

Ivy nodded, her expression grave. "I think the dark force that my great-grandmother wrote about has returned. And I think it's already affecting Lily."

Mrs. Thatcher's face paled slightly, but she remained calm. "Show me what you've found."

Ivy spread the journals out on the table, pointing to the passages that described the dark force and the signs of its presence. Mrs. Thatcher read them carefully, her brow furrowed in concentration.

After a long silence, she looked up at Ivy. "This is indeed troubling. If the seal has been broken, we're dealing with a very dangerous situation. But we still have time. We must gather the coven and reinforce the protective spells. We need to strengthen the bonds that hold this force at bay, and we must do so immediately."

Ivy felt a mix of relief and fear at Mrs. Thatcher's words. The historian's calm demeanor was reassuring, but the gravity of the situation was impossible to ignore. They were about to face an ancient enemy, one that had nearly destroyed the town once before.

As they began planning their next steps, Ivy's thoughts kept drifting back to Lily. She couldn't bear the thought of her best friend being consumed by darkness. Whatever it took, Ivy was determined to save her, even if it meant confronting the force head-on.

The echoes of the past had reached out to warn them, and now it was up to Ivy and the coven to heed that warning and protect Whispers Creek from the gathering storm. The battle ahead would be unlike anything they had faced before, but Ivy knew that with the knowledge of her ancestors and the strength of her friends, they had a chance to prevail.

Chapter 4: *Beneath the Mask*

The sun dipped low in the sky, casting long shadows across Whispers Creek. Ivy and the coven had gathered by the creek, a place where they had always found solace and strength. But tonight, the atmosphere was heavy with tension. The water that usually sparkled in the sunlight now seemed dark and foreboding, reflecting the mood of the group.

Ivy had chosen this spot deliberately, hoping that the familiar surroundings would help Lily open up about what was troubling her. The coven members arranged themselves in a circle on the grass, their faces illuminated by the flickering light of the candles they had brought. The gentle sound of the creek provided a backdrop to the murmured conversations as they waited for Ivy to speak.

Ivy took a deep breath, her heart pounding in her chest. She looked around at her friends, her gaze finally settling on Lily, who sat with her head bowed, her hands clasped tightly in her lap.

"Lily," Ivy began, her voice soft but firm. "We're all worried about you. You've been acting differently, and I feel like there's something you're not telling us."

Lily looked up, her eyes meeting Ivy's. For a moment, there was a flicker of something in her gaze—fear, perhaps, or defiance. Then, she looked away, her expression guarded. "I'm fine, Ivy. I'm just dealing with a lot, that's all."

The words were familiar, but the tone was not. Ivy felt a pang of sadness. This wasn't the Lily she knew, the girl who had stood by her through thick and thin. Something had changed, and Ivy was determined to find out what.

With a glance at Mrs. Thatcher, who nodded encouragingly, Ivy decided to try a more direct approach. "Lily, we think you might be affected by the dark force we've been sensing in town. We want to help you, but we need you to be honest with us."

Lily's shoulders stiffened, and for a moment, Ivy feared she would storm off. But then, to her relief, Lily sighed and nodded. "I know something's wrong," she admitted, her voice barely above a whisper. "I've been having these strange dreams, and I feel like I'm being watched, even when I'm alone."

Ivy reached out and took Lily's hand, giving it a reassuring squeeze. "We're going to get through this together, Lily. We're here for you."

With the rest of the coven's agreement, Ivy proposed a ritual to cleanse Lily of any lingering darkness. They arranged themselves in a circle, Lily at the center, and began the incantation. The air around them hummed with energy as they chanted, their voices rising and falling in a rhythmic cadence.

As the ritual progressed, Ivy felt a surge of hope. The candles flickered, their flames growing brighter as the coven's power intensified. But just as the ritual was reaching its climax, something went wrong. The energy that had been building suddenly faltered, the candles' flames sputtering and dying out.

Lily cried out, her body writhing as if in pain. Ivy and the others rushed to her side, but a force pushed them back, an invisible barrier that they couldn't penetrate. Ivy watched in horror as shadows seemed to swirl around Lily, her features twisted in a mask of agony.

"We have to stop this!" Mrs. Thatcher shouted, her voice cutting through the chaos. Ivy nodded, and together they worked to dismantle the ritual, their hearts heavy with the knowledge that they had failed.

As the last of the candles was extinguished, the shadows around Lily dissipated. She lay on the ground, breathing heavily, her eyes closed. Ivy knelt beside her, tears streaming down her face. She had never felt so helpless.

The coven gathered around Lily, offering what comfort they could. Ivy looked at Mrs. Thatcher, her expression one of determination. "We need to find another way," she said, her voice steady despite the turmoil inside her. "We can't let the darkness win."

Mrs. Thatcher nodded; her eyes filled with understanding. "We'll find a way, Ivy. We'll keep searching until we do."

As the group slowly made their way back to the town, Ivy felt a renewed sense of purpose. The path ahead was uncertain, and the challenges they faced were greater than ever. But she knew that she couldn't give up, not when so much was at stake. The darkness had revealed itself, and now it was up to the coven to confront it, no matter the cost.

Chapter 5: *Whispers in the Dark*

The coven gathered in Ivy's attic, the space that had become their refuge and command center. The atmosphere was tense, the only light coming from the dim glow of the candles placed around the room. After the failed ritual, a sense of urgency had settled over the group. They knew they had to act quickly, but they were unsure of how to proceed.

Ivy sat in the center of the circle, surrounded by the journals and books they had been studying. Her mind was a whirlwind of thoughts, replaying the events of the previous night over and over. Lily had been affected by the dark force, and the coven's usual methods hadn't been enough to help her. They needed a new plan, and they needed it fast.

Mrs. Thatcher cleared her throat, drawing the attention of the group. "I believe our focus should be on finding the source of this darkness," she said, her voice calm but firm. "We need to understand what we're dealing with before we can counteract it effectively."

Noah nodded in agreement. "I've been analyzing the energy readings from the town," he said, pulling out his tablet. "There's a pattern—these fluctuations are originating from a specific area in the woods. It's as if the force is drawing power from that spot."

Claire leaned forward; her eyes filled with concern. "That makes sense. The plants in that area have been behaving strangely, too. I think we should investigate the site and see what we can find."

Ivy listened to her friends, a plan starting to form in her mind. "We'll go tonight," she decided. "We'll take every precaution, but we have to find out what's causing this. "As night fell, the coven made their way through the woods, guided by the light of the full moon. The trees loomed overhead, their branches swaying in the gentle breeze. The air was cool, and the sound of their footsteps seemed to echo in the silence.

Ivy led the way, her senses on high alert. She could feel the energy in the air, a subtle hum that grew stronger as they neared the source. The others followed close behind, their expressions a mix of determination and apprehension.

As they approached the area Noah had identified, Ivy felt a shiver run down her spine. The trees here were different, their bark darker and their leaves wilted. The ground beneath their feet was damp, and the air was thick with the scent of decay.

"This is it," Noah whispered, his eyes fixed on the spot ahead. In the center of the clearing stood a large, ancient oak tree, its gnarled branches reaching out like twisted fingers.

Ivy stepped forward, her heart pounding in her chest. As she reached the base of the tree, she noticed something strange—a faint glow emanating from the roots. She knelt down, brushing away the leaves and dirt to reveal a small, intricately carved stone. The stone pulsed with an eerie light; its surface covered in symbols that Ivy didn't recognize.

Mrs. Thatcher gasped as she saw the stone. "That's a binding stone," she explained, her voice filled with awe. "It was used by the ancient covens to seal away powerful forces. But this one has been tampered with."

Ivy examined the stone closely, her fingers tracing the symbols. "It's been cracked," she observed, her voice tinged with dread. "That's why the darkness has been able to escape."

The realization hit them all at once. The dark force had been imprisoned here, sealed away by a previous coven. But someone had damaged the stone, allowing the darkness to seep out and spread throughout Whispers Creek.

The coven exchanged glances, their resolve strengthening. They knew what they had to do. They needed to repair the stone and reinforce the seal, using the combined power of their magic and the knowledge passed down through generations.

As they prepared to perform the necessary rituals, Ivy felt a renewed sense of hope. They had uncovered the source of the darkness, and now they had a chance to stop it. But they would have to work quickly and carefully, for the darkness was still lurking, waiting for an opportunity to strike.

With a deep breath, Ivy and the coven began their work, their voices rising in unison as they chanted the ancient words. The battle was far from over, but they were ready to face whatever lay ahead. The whispers in the dark would not go unanswered.

Chapter 6: *A Desperate Plan*

Back in Ivy's attic, the air was thick with anticipation as the coven gathered to discuss their next steps. The discovery of the cracked binding stone had been a significant breakthrough, but they knew the real challenge lay ahead. The dark force was still out there, and they needed to find out who had tampered with the stone.

Ivy sat at the center of the room, her eyes scanning the faces of her friends. They looked to her for guidance, and she felt the weight of responsibility on her shoulders. After a moment of silence, she spoke. "We need to perform a ritual to uncover who has been meddling with the binding stone. If we can identify them, we might be able to stop them and repair the damage they've done."

Mrs. Thatcher nodded in agreement. "The ritual we need is complex, but it can be done. We'll need to channel the energy of the stone to trace its connections. This will reveal who has interacted with it."

Noah and Claire began gathering the necessary items for the ritual. They placed the binding stone in the center of the room, surrounded by a circle of candles. Claire added herbs and oils, filling the air with their soothing scents. Noah arranged his instruments to monitor the energy levels, ensuring that they could track any anomalies.

As the coven prepared, Ivy felt a mixture of anxiety and determination. They were stepping into uncharted territory, but she trusted her friends and the strength of their bond. Together, they were stronger than any darkness that might threaten them.

Once everything was in place, Ivy took her position beside the stone. The candles flickered, casting dancing shadows on the walls. She took a deep breath, steadying her nerves. "Are we ready?" she asked, her voice firm.

The coven members nodded, their faces reflecting the gravity of the situation. They joined hands, forming a circle around the stone. Mrs. Thatcher began the incantation, her voice resonating with power. The others followed her lead, their voices blending in harmony.

As they chanted, the stone began to glow, its light pulsing in time with their words. Ivy could feel the energy building, a palpable force that seemed to fill the room. Her senses heightened, and she focused all her attention on the stone, willing it to reveal its secrets.

Suddenly, the room was filled with a brilliant light. The stone vibrated, and images began to form in the air above it—ghostly apparitions that flickered and shifted. The coven watched in awe as the scenes played out before them.

They saw a figure, cloaked in shadows, approaching the binding stone in the dead of night. The figure's features were obscured, but their actions were clear. With deliberate movements, they had cracked the stone, releasing the dark force that had been contained for so long.

As the vision faded, Ivy felt a chill run down her spine. The figure had seemed familiar, but she couldn't place them. She looked at her friends, their expressions mirroring her own confusion and concern.

"We need to find out who that was," Noah said, his voice tense. "They're the key to all of this."

The coven spent the next few hours discussing their options, pouring over the details of the vision and trying to piece together the clues. Ivy's mind raced, sifting through memories and possibilities. She knew they were running out of time. The dark force was growing stronger, and they needed to act before it was too late.

"We should talk to the townspeople," Claire suggested. "Someone might recognize the figure, or know something that could help us."

Ivy nodded. "We'll split up and start asking around. But we need to be careful—if the person responsible realizes we're onto them, they might try to stop us."

As the coven prepared to leave, Ivy felt a surge of determination. They had come too far to back down now. The stakes were higher than ever, but they were ready to face whatever challenges lay ahead. With a last look at the binding stone, she led her friends out of the attic and into the night, their footsteps echoing with the promise of a new beginning.

Chapter 7: *Battle of Wills*

The morning sun filtered through the trees as Ivy and the coven gathered at the town square, each of them charged with a mission. The air was crisp, and the scent of autumn leaves filled the air, but the mood among the friends was tense. After the vision of the cloaked figure tampering with the binding stone, they knew the gravity of their situation. Whoever had damaged the stone was still at large, and their motives were unclear.

Ivy addressed the group, her voice steady and resolute. "We need to talk to as many people as we can. Keep your eyes and ears open. We're looking for anything unusual—someone acting out of character or any rumors about strange behavior. Be discreet but thorough."

Each member of the coven nodded in understanding before dispersing into the town. Ivy paired up with Mrs. Thatcher, and they headed towards the library, a hub for the town's gossip and news. The library's aged wooden doors creaked as they entered, and the familiar scent of old books greeted them.

Inside, the librarian, Mrs. Wexley, greeted them with a warm smile. "Good morning, Ivy, Mrs. Thatcher. What brings you here so early?"

Ivy returned the smile, trying to appear casual. "We're looking into some town history and folklore. Have you heard of anyone unusual or anything odd happening lately?"

Mrs. Wexley leaned over the counter, her eyes sparkling with curiosity. "You know, I've heard whispers of someone sneaking around the woods at night. Old Mr. Crowley claims he saw a shadowy figure by the creek a few nights ago."

Mrs. Thatcher raised an eyebrow. "Did he say who it might be?"

Mrs. Wexley shook her head. "He didn't get a clear look. Said it was too dark and the figure was too quick. But he was certain it wasn't one of the usual folks who visit the creek."

Ivy exchanged a glance with Mrs. Thatcher, a silent understanding passing between them. They thanked Mrs. Wexley and stepped outside, their minds racing with possibilities.

Meanwhile, Claire and Noah were at the general store, chatting with the shopkeeper, Mr. Jenkins. He was a wealth of local knowledge, always in tune with the town's comings and goings.

"I heard about someone buying large quantities of candles and salt," Mr. Jenkins mentioned, scratching his chin. "Seemed odd, especially since they were a stranger to me."

Claire and Noah thanked him and hurried back to the square, where they regrouped with the others. As they shared their findings, a clearer picture began to form. Whoever was behind the disturbance was methodical and cautious, but their actions were starting to leave a trail.

"We should check the woods again tonight," Ivy suggested, her voice firm. "If they've been seen by the creek, they might return."

As night fell, the coven positioned themselves strategically around the creek, hidden among the trees and bushes. The moon cast a silvery glow over the water, and the forest was eerily silent, save for the occasional rustle of leaves in the breeze.

Hours passed with no sign of the mysterious figure. Just as some of them were starting to lose hope, Ivy spotted a shadow moving stealthily along the creek's edge. She signaled to the others, and they watched as the figure approached the ancient oak.

Noah moved closer, trying to get a better look. Suddenly, he stumbled on a branch, and the noise startled the figure, who turned sharply. The hood fell back, revealing a face familiar to them all—Thomas, a quiet and reserved member of the town council.

Thomas's eyes widened in surprise and then narrowed in anger as he realized he'd been caught. "You don't understand," he hissed, backing away. "This is for the good of the town."

Ivy stepped forward, her voice calm but commanding. "What have you done, Thomas? Why did you break the binding stone?"

Thomas's face twisted with a mix of fear and defiance. "The town has been stagnating. I thought if I released some of the energy, we could harness it, use it to bring prosperity back."

"You've put everyone in danger!" Mrs. Thatcher exclaimed. "That force was contained for a reason."

As the coven closed in, Thomas's resolve seemed to waver. He looked around, seeing the determination in their faces. "I didn't mean for it to go this far," he admitted, his voice cracking. "I'll help you fix it."

As Thomas began to explain his plan, a figure emerged from the shadows—Lily. Her eyes were distant, her expression unnervingly calm.

Without warning, Lily raised her hand, and a dark energy crackled in the air. Before anyone could react, a bolt of darkness shot from her fingers, striking Thomas in the chest. He staggered, his eyes wide with shock, before collapsing to the ground.

The coven gasped in horror as Ivy rushed to Thomas's side, but it was too late. The life had already left his eyes.

"Lily, what have you done?" Ivy cried, tears streaming down her face.

Lily looked at her, a cruel smile playing on her lips. "It's necessary, Ivy. The dark force needs a host, and now it's me. Together, we'll bring this town the power it deserves."

Ivy stared at her friend, her heart breaking. The darkness had fully consumed Lily, and she was no longer the girl they knew. The coven exchanged a determined look; they had lost Lily to the darkness, but they wouldn't let it consume their town.

The coven gathered around; their resolve stronger than ever. They knew they had a new enemy to face, one who was once their friend. Ivy's voice was firm as she addressed her friends.

"We need to stop Lily and the dark force within her. We can't let this darkness spread any further."

As they prepared to confront Lily, Ivy knew this would be their greatest challenge yet. The battle for Whispers Creek had become a battle of wills with her best friend, and the fate of their town rested in their hands.

Chapter 8: *The Final Confrontation*

The woods surrounding the town of Whispers Creek were cloaked in an unnatural darkness as Ivy and the coven surrounded Lily by the ancient oak. The air was heavy with tension, the forest eerily silent except for the crunching of leaves beneath their feet.

Lily, once a cherished friend, had become a vessel for the dark force, and it was up to Ivy and her companions to stop her. As they confronted Lily, Ivy's mind raced with the memories of their past, the good times they had shared. The thought of facing Lily in battle was almost unbearable, but she knew it was necessary.

"Ivy," Mrs. Thatcher whispered, placing a reassuring hand on her shoulder. "We're with you. We can do this."

Ivy nodded, drawing strength from the support of her friends. She took a deep breath, steeling herself for the confrontation.

"You shouldn't have come," Lily's voice echoed through the clearing, cold and distant. "This power is mine now, and I won't let you take it from me."

Noah stepped forward, his voice firm. "Lily, this isn't you. The darkness is controlling you. We can help you fight it."

Lily laughed, a sound that sent chills down their spines. "You're wrong, Noah. I've never felt so alive. This power is exactly what I needed to bring change to this town."

Without another word, Lily raised her hands, and a wave of dark energy erupted from her fingertips. The coven scattered, narrowly avoiding the attack. Ivy ducked behind a tree, her heart pounding in her chest.

"Stay focused!" Mrs. Thatcher called out, her voice cutting through the chaos. "We need to find a way to weaken the connection between Lily and the dark force."

As the battle raged on, Ivy racked her brain, trying to think of a solution. Her thoughts were a whirlwind of memories and emotions, but then, something clicked. The pocket watch—the mysterious heirloom she had carried with her throughout their journey. She had completely forgotten about it.

Ivy reached into her pocket, her fingers closing around the familiar shape of the watch. It was warm to the touch, pulsating with a faint glow. She remembered the words of Mrs. Thatcher: "This watch holds the power of time. Use it wisely."

As Lily prepared to unleash another wave of dark energy, Ivy stepped forward, holding the watch aloft. "Lily, I know you're in there. Remember who you are!"

The watch began to glow brighter, its light cutting through the darkness like a beacon. Lily hesitated, her eyes flickering with confusion. The coven watched in awe as the light from the watch enveloped Lily, forming a protective barrier around her.

For a brief moment, the darkness receded, and Lily's eyes returned to their natural color. She looked at Ivy, tears streaming down her face. "Ivy, I'm so sorry. I didn't mean for any of this to happen."

Ivy smiled, her own eyes brimming with tears. "It's okay, Lily. We're going to fix this together."

But the dark force wasn't ready to give up. With a furious roar, it surged forward, attempting to reclaim its hold on Lily. Ivy tightened her grip on the watch, channeling all her energy into the glowing artifact.

The coven gathered around Ivy, joining hands and focusing their collective power. The watch pulsed with a brilliant light, and a wave of energy radiated outward, pushing back the darkness.

Slowly but surely, the dark force began to weaken, its hold on Lily loosening. With one final burst of light, the watch shattered, sending shards of light cascading through the air. The darkness dissolved, and Lily collapsed into Ivy's arms, exhausted but free.

As the sun rose over the clearing, the coven breathed a collective sigh of relief. They had faced the darkness and emerged victorious; their bonds stronger than ever. Ivy cradled the broken pieces of the pocket watch in her hands, a symbol of their triumph and the power of friendship.

"We did it," she whispered, looking at her friends. "We saved Lily and our town."

Mrs. Thatcher placed a comforting hand on Ivy's shoulder. "Yes, we did. But remember, Ivy, this is only the beginning. There will always be challenges, but we'll face them together."

As they made their way back to Whispers Creek, Ivy felt a sense of peace. The battle had been won, but the journey of the Keepers of Time was far from over. Together, they were ready to face whatever the future held.

When they reached the town, a sense of calm and renewal was evident. The townspeople, having heard of the coven's success, gathered around, their faces a mix of relief and gratitude. Mrs. Thatcher looked at Ivy, her eyes filled with pride and a hint of sadness.

"Ivy," she said, her voice wavering slightly, "it's time for me to step down as the leader of the coven and the town historian. You've proven yourself more than capable. The future of Whispers Creek belongs to you now."

Ivy was taken aback, her eyes welling up with emotion. "Mrs. Thatcher, I don't know what to say. You've guided us through so much."

Mrs. Thatcher smiled; her eyes misty. "It's been my honor, Ivy. Watching you grow, seeing the strength and wisdom you've shown... I couldn't be more proud. This town is in good hands with you."

With Ivy at the helm, the town began to heal. The buildings seemed to stand a little taller, the air felt a little lighter, and the creek flowed with a renewed vigor. Whispers Creek was on the path to recovery, and with the Keepers of Time watching over it, the town's future looked bright.

www.ingramcontent.com/pod-product-compliance
Lightning Source LLC
Chambersburg PA
CBHW051308160726
47994CB00003B/1372